A STRANGE SIGHTING

There was a large crowd hanging out behind the wooden barricades, just like there had been the day before. Frank caught sight of their friends among the crowd.

They weren't watching the shoot. They were passing something around.

Frank and Joe walked over to them. "Hey, guys, what's up?" Frank called out curiously.

"Frank! Joe! Where have you been?" Phil exclaimed.

"You won't believe what happened to Madison," Chet added.

Frank turned to Madison. "What's going on? Are you okay?"

"No, I'm *not* okay," Madison replied in a shaky voice. "I saw a zombie this morning. A *real* zombie!"

CATCH UP ON ALL THE HARDY BOYS® SECRET FILES

THE HARDY BOYS®

SECRET FILES #12

Lights, Camera . . . Zombies!

BY FRANKLIN W. DIXON

ILLUSTRATED BY SCOTT BURROUGHS

ALADDIN · NEW YORK LONDON TORONTO SYDNEY NEW DELHI

🪔ALADDIN

An imprint of Simon & Schuster Children's Publishing Division
1230 Avenue of the Americas, New York, NY 10020
First Aladdin paperback edition August 2013
Copyright © 2013 by Simon & Schuster, Inc.
All rights reserved, including the right of reproduction in whole or in part in any form.
ALADDIN is a trademark of Simon & Schuster, Inc., and related logo is a registered trademark of Simon & Schuster, Inc.
THE HARDY BOYS is a registered trademark of Simon & Schuster, Inc.
For information about special discounts for bulk purchases, please contact Simon & Schuster Special Sales at 1-866-506-1949 or business@simonandschuster.com.
The Simon & Schuster Speakers Bureau can bring authors to your live event. For more information or to book an event contact the Simon & Schuster Speakers Bureau at 1-866-248-3049 or visit our website at www.simonspeakers.com.
The text of this book was set in Garamond.
Manufactured in the United States of America 0114 OFF
10 9 8 7 6 5 4 3 2
Library of Congress Control Number 2013935599
ISBN 978-1-4424-5369-2
ISBN 978-1-4424-5370-8 (eBook)

CONTENTS

1

Humans for Lunch

Frank Hardy staggered across the lawn toward his brother, Joe, his arms outstretched. Frank was a zombie, and Joe was a human.

Translation: Joe was Frank's lunch.

Joe, who was a year younger than Frank, picked up a long blue noodle from a pile of pool toys and wielded it like a sword. "You'll never get me!" he cried out.

Frank ignored Joe's threats and continued staggering.

"Stay back, you evil monster!" Joe shook the noodle menacingly at Frank.

Ha-ha, poor Joe. The flimsy foam tube was no match for Zombie Frank's supernatural strength and appetite.

Nearby, Cissy Zermeño staggered toward Tico Sanchez. She was a zombie too, and Tico was *her* lunch.

"I . . . am . . . going . . . to . . . eat . . . you," Cissy growled at Tico.

"Wait! Time-out!" Tico made a *T* with his hands. "You're doing this all wrong, Cissy. Zombies can't talk."

Cissy stopped in her tracks and put her hands on her hips. "Well, *this* zombie can," she said defensively.

Tico shook his head. "No way. Zombies are reanimated flesh. All they can do is move, make moaning noises, and eat people."

"How do you know, Tico? Zombies aren't even real," Frank said, returning to human mode.

"Yeah. Why can't we pretend some zombies can talk?" Joe piped up.

"I'm an expert on zombies. And I've never heard of a zombie that can talk," Tico said. "Besides, do you have *proof* they aren't real? How do you know there aren't zombies right here in Bayport?"

"Um . . . I don't think so." Frank loved zombies, werewolves, and other supernatural creatures as much as the next nine-year-old. But they were totally fictional. It was fun to make believe they existed, though.

Frank, Joe, Cissy, and Tico were playing zombies in the Hardys' backyard. Tico had just moved into the neighborhood. He would be joining the other kids at Bayport Elementary when school started in the fall.

The Hardys' friend Phil Cohen was supposed to be here too, but he was late. Frank wondered where he was.

"Okay, puny humans. Watch and learn," Tico said.

He ruffled his spiky dark brown hair so it was sticking out. He hung his right arm down at his side so that it was lower than his left, making him lopsided. He contorted his face into a monstrous grimace.

With slow, shuffling steps he limped toward Cissy, dragging his left leg behind him. "Ohhhh-hhhhh!" he moaned in a spooky voice. A round silver key chain swung back and forth rhythmically from a belt loop on his black jeans. It had a picture of a zombie on it.

"Whoa! He's really good," Joe whispered to Frank.

Frank nodded. "He's like that psycho zombie in that movie we saw last summer. What was it called?"

"*The Zombie That Ate Chicago*," Joe reminded him.

"Yeah, that's the one." Frank remembered watching it at a sleepover at their friend Chet Morton's house. Frank had covered his eyes during several scary scenes. At one point, during an especially gross part, he had excused himself to go to the bathroom, even though he hadn't needed to.

"Are you zombies ready for some people food?" Mrs. Hardy called out.

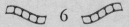

Frank glanced over his shoulder. His mom walked across the lawn carrying a tray piled high with sandwiches. Aunt Gertrude followed behind with a pitcher of lemonade and cups.

Aunt Gertrude was the boys' father's sister. She used to live in New York City. Mr. and Mrs. Hardy had invited her to come live with them.

At first Frank and Joe had been nervous about having a new addition to the family, especially Aunt Gertrude, who could be a little bossy. But it had turned out to be nice to have her around— most of the time. She was a big help with house-work and stuff.

Frank, Joe, Cissy, and Tico raced to the picnic table and sat down. Mrs. Hardy passed out paper plates and napkins, and Aunt Gertrude began pouring lemonade into cups.

"P-B-and-J me, please," Joe said cheerfully.

"Not with those yucky zombie paws, you

don't," Aunt Gertrude chided him. She thrust a packet of antibacterial wipes at him.

"But they're not dirty!" Joe protested, holding up his hands.

"That's what you always say, young man," Aunt Gertrude observed drily. "Take a wipe and pass it around the table, please."

Sighing, Joe obeyed.

"Where's Phil? I made enough sandwiches for five of you," Mrs. Hardy asked.

"I'm not sure. He was supposed to be here, like, half an hour ago," Frank said.

Joe shrugged. "He's probably building a computer from scratch and lost track of the—"

"*Guys!* Guess what?"

Everyone looked up. It was Phil—finally! His face was red and he was out of breath, as though he had been running.

"Phil, you're just in time for lunch. Do you

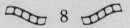 8

want tuna salad, ham and cheese, or peanut butter and jelly?" Mrs. Hardy asked.

Phil slid onto the bench next to Frank. "Thanks, Mrs. Hardy, but I'm too excited to eat," he gasped. "I just heard the most amazing news ever. Raj Kureshi is in Bayport!"

"*No. Way.*" Tico's eyes grew enormous.

"That's awesome!" Frank exclaimed. Raj Kureshi was a famous Hollywood director whose specialty was sci-fi and horror movies. Frank's personal favorites were *Vampires Versus Robots* and *They Came From Jupiter.*

Phil grinned. "I haven't even told you guys the best part. He's shooting a movie here. And it's going to be about zombies!"

2

Lights, Camera, Zombies!

Move over. You're blocking my view," Joe told Adam Ackerman.

"No, you're blocking *my* view," Adam said. He popped a piece of Monster Melon bubble gum into his mouth and elbowed Joe, not gently.

Joe sighed and tried to move to a better spot— far away from Adam, who was a big bully and not fun to be around. But it was nearly impossible. Everyone in town seemed to have turned

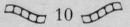

up in Bayport Park for the first day of the *Zombie Mania* shoot. The crowd jostled against the line of wooden barriers, trying to peek at the set and take pictures of celebrities.

The man in front of Joe leaned down to tie his sneaker. *Yes!* All of a sudden Joe had an almost perfect view of the set.

Craning his neck, Joe gazed around East Meadow in awe. The place was a beehive of activity. Dozens of people—crew members?—ran around with walkie-talkies and silver clipboards.

Other people hung out inside large tents. Joe thought he recognized Raj Kureshi among them. He remembered the director's shiny bald head and black-framed glasses from a TV interview.

There was equipment everywhere too: big cameras poised on tripods (except these tripods had more than three legs); massive lights; ladders, cranes, and scaffolds like the ones at construction sites; and long poles with what looked like microphones attached to them.

Then the man in front of Joe finished tying his shoe and stood up. *Show over.*

"Joe! Over here!"

Joe turned around. Frank waved to him from the far edge of the crowd. Next to him were Cissy, Phil, Tico, Chet Morton, and Chet's sister Iola. There were a bunch of other kids from school there too, including Madison, Melissa, and Melissa's brother, Todd.

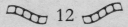

12

Joe frowned. How could they see anything from way back there?

Frank waved to him again. Mumbling "Excuse me," Joe made his way toward his brother and their schoolmates.

"This is the perfect spot," Frank said to Joe when he reached them. "If you stand on your toes and lean way to the left, you can sort of see inside the tent where they're doing hair and makeup. That's where the actors and actresses are."

"The tall blond actress who's playing the zombie mom? My dad and I saw her at the grocery store yesterday," Chet spoke up. "She was buying cereal! I said hi, and she smiled at me!"

"Big deal. The actor who plays Zog the zombie hunter? My dad's cousin's best friend's neighbor went to college with him," Madison bragged.

Madison was the most popular girl in their school. She was surrounded by her usual entourage

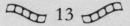

of admirers. They all looked at her, wide-eyed, and a girl named Beatrice murmured, "Ohmigosh, Madison, you know *everyone!*"

Rolling his eyes, Joe stood on his toes and leaned way to the left, like Frank had said. *Hmm.* There *was* kind of a decent view of the hair and makeup tent. Joe watched, fascinated, as a woman smeared purple and yellow goop onto an actor's face.

"Where are the zombies?" Chet asked, confused.

"Uh, duh? That's what those people in that tent are doing," Tico said. "They're hair and makeup experts. They work hours and hours to turn those actors and actresses into zombies. Plus, the actors still have to get into their zombie costumes."

"Oh, wow! There's Raj Kureshi!" Cissy said, pointing.

Joe followed her finger. The director strode

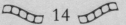 14

briskly toward one of the cameras. Beside him was a woman with short black hair. She looked very businesslike in a beige suit and high heels. She said something to him, and his face creased into a deep frown.

Then Joe noticed a little girl skipping behind the two of them. She wore a red superhero cape over her yellow sundress, and a headband with ladybug antennae.

The girl tugged on Mr. Kureshi's shirt and said something. The director turned around and said something back. The girl pouted unhappily.

"I wonder if that girl's an actress," Joe said out loud.

Madison flipped her hair over her shoulder. "Nope. That's his daughter, Roma. She's five. I've seen her picture in *Celebrity* magazine."

Madison's friend Haley smiled at her in admiration. "Madison, you are so smart!"

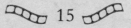

"Madison, you are so smart!" Joe mimicked under his breath. Frank grinned.

There was a faint buzzing sound. Madison reached into her pocket and pulled out her cell phone. It vibrated with a new text message.

Madison stared at the screen and gasped.

"*Oh. My. Gosh.* News flash, people! My mom just texted. She found out that Raj Kureshi is going to hire a couple of local kids for the movie!"

"To do what?" Beatrice asked her.

"To be zombie extras. The parts are super-small, but still! Mom said the casting call is on Friday." Madison frowned at her phone. "Casting call—what is that?"

Melissa stepped forward. "I'm sure that none of you amateurs know what a casting call is," she said smugly. "It's the same thing as auditions or tryouts. But Mr. Kureshi shouldn't even bother. Todd and I are totally getting those parts!"

3

A Zombie Sighting

Frank and Joe exchanged a glance. Melissa and Todd thought they were famous actors, even though they weren't. They had starred in a commercial once for Tasty, Tasty Treats Ice Cream, and they always managed to score the leads in the school plays.

"What makes you so sure?" Cissy asked Melissa. "I bet a bunch of kids are going to try out for those parts."

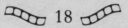

"So what? None of them are Hollywood pros like Todd and me," Melissa bragged. "Right, Todd?"

Hollywood pros? Seriously? Frank thought.

"Uh, right." Behind her, Todd blushed and glanced down at his feet. He seemed uncomfortable with his sister's bragging.

"Well, *I'm* going to try out," Phil said.

"Me too. It would be so cool to be in a movie!" Iola said.

All of a sudden everyone was buzzing about the news. Frank turned to Joe. "Do you think we should try out too?" he said in a low voice.

"Are you kidding? *Yes,*" Joe replied immediately. "You and me playing zombies in a Raj Kureshi movie? That would be, like, the most epic experience ever!"

Frank smiled. His brother was right.

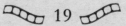 19

The question was: How were they going to beat out all this competition?

On Tuesday morning Frank and Joe sat in front of the family computer in their pajamas. They were reading an online article called "How to Become a Movie Extra"—for about the tenth time.

"I still don't understand some of this stuff. Like, what's an A.D.?" Joe asked Frank.

"I think A.D.s and assistant directors are the same thing," Frank guessed. "It sounds like A.D.s do a bunch of important stuff. Like helping out with hiring extras."

Joe nodded. "Cool. And do we bring our own zombie costumes for the tryout? I mean, casting call? Or do they give us one?"

"This article says we should ask the A.D.s about that. But we should bring costumes, just to be safe," Frank replied.

"Smart." Joe reached for a half-eaten granola bar that was sitting on the desk. "Is this mine or yours? I'm starving."

Frank made a face. "I think that's yours, from yesterday. Or maybe the day before. It's probably infested with ants."

"Ha-ha," Joe said, taking a big bite.

Fenton Hardy walked into the room. He had a folded-up newspaper in one hand and a cup of coffee in the other. "Maybe you two should join the rest of us in the kitchen and eat a real breakfast," he said merrily. "So. Are you movie stars yet?"

"That's what we're working on, Dad," Joe replied. "We're doing research on how to be extras and stuff."

"And we're doing research on zombies, too," Frank added.

"Sounds good. Research is important." As a private detective and former police officer, Mr. Hardy always did a lot of research for his work. "This zombie movie is certainly getting a lot of press. There's a big article about it in the paper."

"Can we see? Can we see?" Joe asked eagerly.

Mr. Hardy handed him the paper. Joe unfolded it and spread it out over the computer keyboard.

Frank peered over Joe's shoulder. The front-page headline read:

HOLLYWOOD DIRECTOR RAJ KURESHI BRINGS ZOMBIES TO BAYPORT

The article went on to explain that Mr. Kureshi planned to spend several weeks in town to shoot three key scenes for *Zombie Mania*. The movie was scheduled to be released next summer.

There was a small paragraph about the casting call for extras. It said: *A source close to the movie indicated that two or three local residents would be cast for*

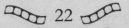 22

small parts in an important scene. The director is looking for boys and girls ages eight to twelve.

Frank mulled this over. "Dad, what does it mean when they say 'a source close to the movie'? What's a source?"

"In this case it's someone who's connected to the movie and has inside information about it," Mr. Hardy explained. "It might be one of the movie's publicists."

"What's a publicist?" Frank asked him.

"A publicist's job is to get everyone excited about a new movie, a new book, a new TV show, that sort of thing. A publicist has to make sure there are a lot of newspaper and magazine articles, online coverage, and so forth." Mr. Hardy added, "I'm sure the *Zombie Mania* people have hired a whole team of publicists. Good publicity is really important to the success of a movie."

"Huh." Joe chomped on his granola bar. "Does

 23

that mean when Raj Kureshi makes Frank and me his extras, the newspapers will write an article about *us*?"

Frank laughed. "Wow, Joe! You're starting to sound just like Melissa," he joked.

Joe didn't look amused.

Later that morning Frank and Joe headed over to East Meadow for day two of the *Zombie Mania* shoot. Frank noticed Raj Kureshi near one of the big tents, talking to a couple of actors in zombie makeup and costumes.

He elbowed Joe and pointed to the actors. "Look!"

"Awesome," Joe said eagerly. "That could be us, like, next week!"

There was a large crowd hanging out behind the wooden barricades, just like there had been the day before. Frank caught sight of their friends among the crowd.

Weird. They weren't watching the shoot. They were passing something around.

Frank and Joe walked over to them. "Hey, guys, what's up?" Frank called out curiously.

"Frank! Joe! Where have you been?" Phil exclaimed.

"You won't believe what happened to Madison," Chet added.

Frank turned to Madison. "What's going on? Are you okay?"

"No, I'm *not* okay," Madison replied in a shaky voice. "I saw a zombie this morning. A *real* zombie!"

4

Strange Footprints

A real zombie? *Yeah, right,* Joe thought. What would Madison claim next? That a UFO had landed in her backyard? That her pet hamster had shape-shifted into a German shepherd?

Joe glanced at Frank. Frank shrugged.

"My mom and I were walking Princess in the park this morning," Madison went on. "That's when I saw him . . . her . . . it."

"Madison has proof!" her friend Haley piped up.

Frank raised his eyebrows. "Proof?"

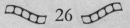

"Yeah." Madison scanned the crowd. "Um, who has my phone?" she called out.

"Here!" An older girl walked over to Madison and handed the phone to her. Joe didn't recognize the girl.

Madison held up her phone for Frank and Joe to see. Joe squinted at the fuzzy photo on the screen. Had Madison been showing it to everyone?

Joe studied the image carefully. Okay, so the person—or thing?—in the photo *did* look like a zombie. The creature had a purplish-yellow face and shoulder-length gray hair that stuck out sloppily from under a white baseball hat. It wore a beige raincoat, green sweatpants, and red-and-black sneakers.

"Where did you take this?" Frank asked Madison curiously.

"On the other side of the park, in West Meadow, near the mayor statue," Madison replied.

The mayor statue? Joe wondered. *Oh, yeah.* Madison

was talking about the statue of Cleavon Finch, former mayor of Bayport.

"Did your mom see the zombie too?" Joe asked Madison.

Madison shook her head. "She was talking to her friend Mrs. Hillman on the phone about some dumb bake sale. I tried to get her attention. But the zombie got away."

Just then Melissa marched up to Madison. "Let me see that picture," she demanded.

"Excuse me?" Madison snapped.

Melissa grabbed the phone from Madison and stared hard at the photo. Her mouth twitched for a second before settling into a smirk. "This is *not* a zombie," she said loudly. "I think it's that guy who works at the library. His name is Ray or Rafe."

"That is totally not that guy," Joe said.

"Yeah, it is! Todd, isn't that Ray or Rafe or whatever?" Melissa asked her brother.

Todd peered at the picture and frowned. "I don't think it's—"

"See? Todd agrees with me," Melissa cut in quickly.

Madison grabbed her phone back from Melissa. "Well, *I* think it was a real zombie," she insisted. "It moved in that slow, creepy way. And it made these creepy moaning noises, too."

"Yeah, right," Melissa said, rolling her eyes.

"Go ahead and make fun of me. But if someone doesn't solve this mystery soon, we could all be in terrible danger!" Madison cried out.

"Did you see the, uh, zombie on this path, or that path?" Frank asked Madison.

Madison hesitated in front of Mayor Cleavon Finch's statue. Just past it the path forked off into a V. Each path went off into the woods.

"Hmm. I don't remember," Madison said after a moment. "It all happened so fast!"

Frank, Madison, Joe, and Chet had gotten permission from their parents to check out Madison's "zombie sighting." Mrs. Hardy had driven the four kids over to West Meadow and was parked nearby, waiting for them. Normally she would have let Frank and Joe walk over on their own. But when Joe had mentioned the word "zombie," she had

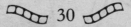

insisted on driving. She had added hastily that there was no such thing as zombies.

"Footprints!" Chet said suddenly. "Zombie footprints, I mean. Look!"

He pointed to the path that went off to the left. There were unusual marks in the dirt. Chet was an expert on tracking. Or rather, tracking was one of his many hobbies.

Frank and Joe went over to inspect the marks. Chet was right. They were footprints. *Strange* footprints.

An imprint of a shoe—a left shoe—was followed by a long, smudgy line, as though someone had dragged his or her right shoe.

Then the pattern repeated again. And again. The prints trailed into the woods and disappeared in a grove of ferns and moss.

Joe glanced around uneasily. Two teenagers walked along, holding hands. A dad strolled by with a sleeping baby. Everything seemed so normal—a typical morning in Bayport Park.

Except for the zombie footprints. If they *were* zombie footprints.

Joe bent down to look more closely at them. Just then he noticed something small and shiny wedged in the dirt.

He picked it up and turned it over in his hand.

"What is it, Joe?" Frank asked.

"It's a clue," Joe said slowly. "I think our zombie may have dropped this!"

5

The Six Ws

A clue?" Frank said excitedly.

He, Madison, and Chet gathered around Joe. Joe held up the small, shiny object.

Frank peered closely at it. It was a key chain with a round silver medallion attached to it. On the silver medallion was an image of a zombie and the words:

ZOMBEE KLUB

Frank frowned. There was something familiar about the key chain.

"Yeah, so I guess our zombie belongs to a club, and they don't know how to spell," Joe joked.

"Guys, this isn't funny! It was a real zombie, I swear!" Madison insisted.

"Iola's friend thought she saw a real zombie

once. But it turned out to be her uncle Henry. He hadn't shaved in, like, three days," Chet piped up.

While Madison and Chet argued about the existence of zombies, Frank pulled Joe aside and pointed to the key chain. "Do you recognize it?" he whispered.

"No. But I feel like we've seen it before," Joe replied.

Frank squeezed his eyes shut, trying to remember. "It was hanging from someone's pocket or something," he murmured.

"Tico!" Joe burst out. "That day we were playing zombies in our backyard. There was a silver zombie key chain on his belt loop!"

Frank opened his eyes. "Oh, yeah. That's right!"

"So Tico was here," Joe concluded.

"Pretending to be a zombie," Frank added.

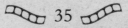 35

"I was *not* in the park this morning pretending to be a zombie!" Tico said hotly.

It was late afternoon on Tuesday. Frank and Joe had walked over to Tico's house to ask him about the Zombee Klub key chain. They had found Tico on his porch, reading comic books.

Before Tico could even say hi, Joe had accused him of being Madison's "zombie." That strategy hadn't worked out so well.

Frank pointed to one of Tico's comic books. "Hey, is that the special anniversary edition of 'Zombie Kingdom'?" he said in a friendly voice.

"Yeah." Tico's eyes lit up. "I stood in line at the comic book store on the day it came out, to make sure I got a copy."

Tico is definitely obsessed with zombies, Frank thought. "Look. It's no big deal if you walked around the park dressed up like a zombie," he said lightly.

"Yeah. Frank showed up to school dressed up like a green space alien once," Joe piped up.

Frank was about to object; he had never showed up to school dressed up like a green space alien! Then he realized Joe was trying to get Tico to confess. Frank kept his mouth shut.

Unfortunately, Tico kept his mouth shut too. He wasn't talking.

Frank reached into his pocket and pulled out the silver key chain. "This is yours, right?"

Tico startled. "Hey, where'd you find that? I thought I lost it!"

"We found it in the park. It was on the path, right by those fake zombie footprints you made," Joe replied.

Tico was silent. He took the key chain from

Frank and rubbed some dirt off it with his thumb. "Look. I did go over there today," he said after a moment. "But I wasn't Madison's zombie!"

"Oh, yeah? What were you doing there, then?" Joe demanded.

"I was one of the first people at the *Zombie Mania* shoot this morning," Tico explained. "Madison showed up right after me, with a couple of her super-annoying friends. She told everyone about seeing a zombie in West Meadow. I was curious, so I snuck away to check it out myself."

"Did you see anything when you were there? Or anyone?" Frank asked him.

Tico shook his head. "Just those footprints. I guess I dropped my key chain while I was poking around."

"Or else you dropped your key chain while you were pretending to be a zombie," Joe said.

"I told you, that wasn't me!" Tico protested.

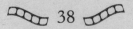

Frank stared at Tico and tried to read his expression.

Was Tico telling the truth? Or was he lying?

After dinner Frank and Joe headed over to their top secret tree house with a couple of cherry Popsicles. The tree house was hidden halfway up a very tall old maple in the woods bordering the Hardys' backyard. The only way to get up to it was by a ladder attached to a rope and pulley.

The boys pulled down the ladder and climbed up. The inside of the tree house was one big room furnished with a couple of beanbag chairs on the wooden floor. Posters of martial arts and monster movies covered one wall, and a dry-erase whiteboard hung on another.

Joe plopped down on a cushion and ate his Popsicle, which had started to melt in the summer heat. Frank thought that his brother kind of looked like a zombie himself, with red dripping from his mouth.

"Okay, so let's catch this zombie," Joe said eagerly. "You're going to list the six *W*s, right?"

"Right." Frank walked up to the whiteboard and picked up a marker. The six *W*s was a system he and Joe had developed while watching their father solve his own mysteries. They'd been using the system for a while now. It was technically five *W*s and one *H*, but it was a lot easier to call it the six *W*s.

Frank wrote:

Who: Tico

What: He pretended to be a zombie.

When: Tuesday morning

Where: Bayport Park, West Meadow,
    near the mayor statue

Why: ???

How: He put on zombie clothes and
    makeup and left zombie footprints
    in the dirt.

Frank wasn't sure what to fill in for the Why. "Okay, so . . . why would Tico pretend to be a zombie, then lie about it?" he said out loud.

"If he *was* lying. He might have been telling the truth," Joe pointed out.

"Yeah." Frank thought about it for a moment, then wrote: *Zombie obsession???* after the Why.

Just then they heard someone coming up the ladder. Very few people even knew about the tree house. Frank wondered who it could be.

After a second, Chet's head popped up through the opening in the floor.

"Hey, Chet," Frank said, surprised. "What are you doing here?"

"I had to tell you guys right away," Chet said breathlessly. "You know Madison's picture? Of that zombie?"

"Yeah?" Joe said.

"It's all over the news!" Chet announced.

6

Monstersightings.com

Inside the Hardys' house Joe, Frank, and Chet gathered around the family computer. Aunt Gertrude brought them a plate of freshly baked chocolate chip cookies and glasses of cold milk, then settled down on the couch to read a magazine.

Score! Joe thought, grabbing a cookie. Obviously Aunt Gertrude didn't know about the Popsicles the boys had eaten earlier. She wasn't big on multiple desserts after dinner.

"Okay. So do a search for 'zombie sighting' and

'Bayport,'" Chet told Frank, whose fingers were poised over the keyboard.

Frank typed. After a few seconds a long list of links came up on the screen.

He clicked on the first link. It led to a website called Monstersightings.com. A headline on the home page blared:

ZOMBIE SIGHTING IN BAYPORT!

Just below the headline was Madison's fuzzy zombie photo.

"That is so random," Joe said, puzzled. "How did Monstersightings.com get hold of Madison's picture?"

"They're not the only ones," Chet said. "I'm telling you, it's on a gazillion websites!"

"Huh." Joe munched on his cookie and scanned the Monstersightings.com article:

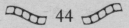

This morning a Bayport resident reported seeing a zombie in the local park. She was able to take this photo with her cell phone before the creature fled into the forest. A source close to the situation was quoted as saying: "Some people refuse to believe zombies exist. But I'm definitely locking my doors tonight!"

Posted Tuesday 5:15 p.m. by Luke Johnson

"'Source close to the situation'? *What* source?" Joe said out loud. He remembered what their dad had said this morning about sources and publicists and all that.

"A friend of Madison's, maybe?" Frank guessed.

"Or maybe it was Madison herself," Joe mused.

"Huh?" Chet sounded totally confused.

Joe reached for his third cookie. Aunt Gertrude glanced up from her magazine and frowned at him.

 45

"Yeah. So maybe Madison faked that zombie picture and spread it around," Joe said. "You know, to get attention. Madison *loves* attention."

Frank nodded. "I think it's time to add Madison to our suspect list."

"Definitely," Joe agreed.

On Wednesday morning Madison was surrounded by her usual group of admirers at the *Zombie Mania* shoot.

"Madison, you're famous!" Beatrice cried out.

"Your picture is everywhere!" Haley piped up.

Joe watched Madison, expecting her to gloat and say something obnoxious. But instead she fidgeted and seemed uncomfortable. What was up with that?

He and Frank went up to her. "Hey, Madison? Can we talk to you?" Frank asked her.

"Alone?" Joe added.

Madison blinked nervously. "Um, I guess?" She turned to her friends and said, "I'll be right back."

Madison followed Frank and Joe over to a secluded spot under a willow tree.

"So, how does it feel to be, uh, famous?" Joe asked Madison.

Madison's eyes welled up with tears. "It's awful!" she blurted out.

"What? Why?" Frank said, surprised.

"My parents are really mad at me about the zombie picture," Madison said, her lip quivering. "I'm not allowed to use the computer or watch TV for a whole week. It's so unfair!"

"You mean they're mad at you for taking the picture? Or for posting it all over the Internet?" Joe asked her.

"I did *not* post it all over the Internet. Someone else did. But my parents won't believe me," Madison complained.

 47

Joe regarded her. She seemed genuinely upset. *Hmmm.* "Well, if you didn't post it, then who did?"

"Yeah. Did you text it to someone? Like one of your friends?" Frank added.

"No! I'm not allowed to text pictures," Madison replied.

Joe remembered that Madison had been passing her phone around yesterday morning and sharing her zombie picture with the crowd. In theory anyone there could have texted it. "Madison, can I see your phone?"

"Sure." Madison reached into her pocket and handed her phone to Joe.

Joe wasn't an expert on cell phones—unlike Phil, who knew everything there was to know about high-tech gadgets. But Joe could figure out the basics, like if Madison's zombie photo had been texted, and to what number.

Joe scrolled around until he found the information he needed. The photo had been texted to a number with an out-of-state area code yesterday at 10:01 a.m.

Joe showed the number to Madison. "Do you recognize it?" he asked her.

Madison shook her head. "N-no. I've never seen that number before."

"I know! Let's call it," Frank suggested.

"Yeah, let's!" Joe hit the call button.

The phone rang once and then went straight to a voice mail recording: "This is Vanessa. Leave a message!" *Beeeeep!*

Joe hung up quickly. "Who's Vanessa?" he asked Madison.

Madison frowned. "Vanessa? I don't know anyone named Vanessa." Her face lit up. "Oh, yeah. My mom's hairstylist's name is Vanessa!" She frowned again. "Or is it Vivian? Or Veronica? Or maybe it's *Janessa*, with a *J*."

"Great," Frank mumbled.

Dogs began barking to the tune of "Twinkle, Twinkle, Little Star." Joe realized with a start that it was the ringtone on Madison's phone. Joe wondered if Mystery Vanessa was dialing Madison's number to find out who had called her a second ago.

But the screen flashed: *MOM CALLING*.

"Uh, it's your mom," Joe said, handing the phone back to Madison.

Madison glanced at the screen and hit talk. "Hi, Mommy. . . . *What?* No, I didn't talk to a reporter named Luke Jackson. . . . What? No, I didn't talk to a Luke *Johnson*, either. . . ."

Frank tugged on Joe's arm and pulled him aside. "You and I got to the *Zombie Mania* shoot at, like, ten thirty yesterday," he said in a low voice. "I remember looking at my watch. Madison got here earlier. Like, before ten. So someone in the crowd could have grabbed her phone and texted the picture to this Vanessa person at ten or so." He added, "*Or* Vanessa could have texted it to herself. To her own phone, I mean."

"Makes sense," Joe agreed. "Maybe we should add Vanessa to our suspect list—whoever she is."

"We're missing a Why, though. Why would Vanessa post that picture all over the Internet?

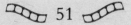 51

Was she Luke Johnson's 'source'? Why would she say that stuff to him for his article?" Frank mused.

"Frank! Joe!"

The boys turned around. Cissy ran up to them.

"What's wrong?" Joe asked her. She looked shaken.

"I just saw a zombie in the park. It tried to attack me!" she cried out.

7

Too Many Zombies

O kay, *where* did you see this zombie?" Frank asked Cissy.

"I think we're almost there," Cissy replied.

Cissy led the way through Bayport Park on a wide jogging path lined with wildflowers. Frank and Joe flanked her on the right and left. Every few seconds, joggers and exercise walkers passed by. It was a beautiful morning, perfect for a run or stroll in the park.

Frank felt uneasy, though. Unlike Madison, Cissy wasn't the sort of person to make up a zombie story for attention. If Cissy said she'd seen a zombie, she had seen a zombie. Or at least someone *pretending* to be a zombie.

This case is getting weirder by the minute, Frank thought.

"I don't know, guys. Maybe this isn't safe. Maybe we should call the police and let *them* catch the zombie," Cissy said anxiously.

Frank glanced around. "I think we're okay. There are a lot of people here."

"Yeah. That zombie can't eat *all* of us," Joe joked. Cissy turned pale. "Just kidding!" he added quickly.

"Really, Joe?" Frank said with a sigh. Was his brother that clueless? Cissy was freaked out enough already.

Frank turned to Cissy. "So, what did this, uh,

zombie look like? Was it like the zombie in Madison's picture?"

"No, it was different from that one," Cissy said. "It was tall with big shoulders. Its face was all gross and greenish. Oh, and it was wearing a football jersey. I think there was a name on the back of it. Maybe A-something?"

Frank considered this. The letter *A* was definitely a clue. "Do you remember anything else?"

"Yes! It talked to me. It said"—Cissy dropped her voice to a low, scary moan—"'I . . . am . . . a . . . zombie.'"

"It *talked*?" Joe said incredulously.

"Uh-huh. See, I *told* you they could! Then I ran like crazy. When I looked over my shoulder, it was gone." Cissy was the shortest student in their entire grade, but she was twice as fast as anyone else. She could outrun anyone or anything.

The three of them continued walking in silence. Pretty soon they were at the edge of the woods.

"There!" Cissy said, pointing. "I saw the zombie on the path next to that bench."

Frank and Joe went over to the spot. Unfortunately, there were no visible zombie footprints on the path—or human ones either. Too many people had gone over that area, and their footprints were all jumbled together in the dirt.

But Frank did notice something else—something small, orange, and crumpled. He picked it up and uncrumpled it.

It was a Monster Melon bubble gum wrapper.

Joe plucked the wrapper out of Frank's hand. "Monster Melon!" he exclaimed. "I saw someone chewing this stuff, like, yesterday. Or the day before, maybe."

"Who?" Frank asked eagerly.

Joe scrunched up his face. "It was Adam," he said after a moment. "Adam Ackerman!"

Frank's eyes widened. Could Adam be their zombie?

• • •

At lunchtime Frank and Joe took their sandwiches out to the tree house so they could discuss the case.

As soon as they were settled inside, Frank went up to the whiteboard. He picked up the marker and made two more columns for two more suspects: Madison and Adam. He wrote their names down after *Who*.

Joe took a bite of his ham and cheese sandwich and studied the whiteboard. "The Why is a piece of cake with Adam. He's a jerk!"

"Yeah," Frank agreed. Adam Ackerman was the biggest bully in Bayport. He also loved to pull pranks on people.

Frank turned back to the whiteboard. Next to Adam's Why he wrote: *Adam is a jerk*. Joe grinned and gave a thumbs-up sign.

"I think Adam and Tico are our best suspects," Frank mused. "They could have pretended to be zombies yesterday in West Meadow . . . and today

 59

on the jogging trail." He added, "What about Madison, though? She's still a suspect too. Did she pretend to be a zombie yesterday and take that picture of herself?"

"*Wellll* . . . maybe Beatrice or Haley or one of her other friends took the picture," Joe guessed. "Or maybe one of them pretended to be the zombie and Madison took the picture."

"Yeah, but what about this morning? Cissy said that her zombie was tall with big shoulders," Frank reminded his brother. "Madison doesn't fit that description. Neither do Beatrice or Haley or Madison's other friends."

"Or maybe Tico or Adam was the zombie today *and* yesterday, and Madison took the picture yesterday, like she said. But maybe she was lying about the Internet part. Maybe she *did* post the zombie picture all over the place so she could become famous," Joe rambled.

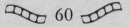 60

Frank tried to record everything on the white-board. He had to use smaller and smaller hand-writing to fit it into the space—and they hadn't even gotten to their fourth possible suspect, Vanessa. "Complicated," he said with a sigh.

"Supercomplicated," Joe agreed. "Plus, don't forget the most important thing!"

"What?" Frank asked him.

Joe tapped his watch. "The casting call is only two days away. We need to practice being zombies, or we'll never get to be extras in the movie!" he pointed out.

"Oh, yeah." Frank stared at the whiteboard. Time was running out. How were they going to get ready for the casting call *and* solve their mystery too?

8

Mystery Vanessa

After lunch Joe and Frank hurried back to the *Zombie Mania* set to try to find Adam. A huge crowd was gathered behind the wooden barricades, watching intensely as Raj Kureshi directed a scene.

In the scene a big, tall zombie chased several screaming campers across the field. A couple of fog machines spewed fake mist, creating a spooky atmosphere.

How awesome is that? Joe thought. Goose bumps pricked his arms.

"Come on, Joe. We have a case to solve," Frank reminded him.

"Yeah, yeah." Joe wished he could just hang out and watch the shoot along with the rest of the crowd. Being a detective was hard work!

Joe and Frank found Adam standing near Tico, Melissa, Todd, and some other kids from school. Frank tapped Adam on the shoulder.

Adam turned around, noisily slurping a bright orange slushie. "What do you want? I'm busy!" he snapped.

"Busy doing what? Pretending to be a zombie?" Joe asked him.

Adam glared at Joe. "Well, at least I'm not pretending to be a detective. Get lost, punks!"

Joe tried to think of something clever and mean

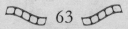

to shoot back at Adam. But he was distracted by a greenish-gray smudge under Adam's nose.

"Hey, Adam? You have a big booger hanging from your nose," Joe said, pointing. "Or else you forgot to clean off all your zombie makeup."

"Huh?" Adam swiped at his nose and glanced at the back of his hand. For a second his eyes flashed with panic. "It's just, uh, some gum. Now leave me alone before I dump this slushie all over your heads!"

"Admit it, Adam! You're the fake zombie in Madison's picture," Frank accused him. "And you faked being a zombie this morning, too, to scare Cissy. In fact—"

Frank was interrupted by Melissa. "I knew it!" she said triumphantly. She had obviously been standing close by and eavesdropping.

Todd hovered behind her, staring at his shoes.

"See, Todd? Didn't I tell you that Adam was the zombie who's been terrorizing Bayport Park?" Melissa said to him.

Todd startled. "What? Um, sure."

All of a sudden Joe noticed that Melissa and Todd both wore black T-shirts that said: ZOMBIE MANIA CAST MEMBERS. "Uh, Melissa? Where did you guys get those T-shirts?" he asked her curiously.

"What? Oh, these silly little things? I had

them made up at the mall," Melissa said casually. "I figured they would come in handy after Todd and I got those parts on Friday."

Todd leaned forward and whispered something into Melissa's ear. Melissa frowned and hissed an angry response. They seemed to be arguing about something.

"*Later!* We will discuss this *later!*" Melissa told Todd. She fake-smiled at Joe, Frank, and Adam. "Soooo. What were we talking about?"

"About how clueless you all are," Adam replied testily. "Okay, so I put on some zombie makeup this morning to try to freak people out. And Cissy happened to be there. Big deal."

"Aha!" Melissa exclaimed.

"But I'm not the zombie in Madison's stupid picture," Adam went on. "I would never wear that lame wig. Or that lame outfit."

"He's obviously lying," Melissa stage-whispered to Frank and Joe.

"I'm *not* lying!" Adam took a menacing step toward Melissa. "Maybe I should dump this slushie on *your* head."

"Don't you dare, you . . . you . . . *Philistine!*" Melissa cried out dramatically.

Adam frowned. "Phili-what?"

Melissa and Adam continued arguing. In the background Todd squirmed uncomfortably.

Joe bent his head toward Frank's. "Okay, so why would Adam tell the truth about being the jogging-trail zombie but lie about being the West Meadow zombie?" he said in a low voice.

"I was thinking the same thing," Frank replied. "Maybe we have two zombies after all?"

Just then, a familiar-looking woman passed by them. She had short black hair and wore a gray business suit. She walked briskly toward the wooden barricades with a fancy cell phone glued to her ear.

"Hi. This is Vanessa," she said to the person on the other end.

Joe did a double take. Did she say her name was Vanessa?

And then he remembered where he'd seen her before. She'd been on the set with Raj Kureshi on the first day of the shoot.

Joe wondered: Could she be *the* Vanessa? Mystery Vanessa?

9

Closing In

Joe started following Vanessa. He motioned for Frank to do the same.

Vanessa continued talking on the phone. "Did you hear about the second zombie sighting in the park? Get on it right away. All this publicity is fabulous for the movie!" she said excitedly.

Joe elbowed Frank. "Did you hear that? She said something about publicity for the movie!" he whispered.

Frank nodded eagerly. He wondered if this

was *the* Vanessa—the one who'd received a text of Madison's zombie picture on Tuesday morning. Was she one of those publicists their dad had told them about?

Vanessa said good-bye to the person on the other end and tucked her phone into her purse. The Hardys rushed up to her.

"Excuse me," Joe said loudly. "We're, uh . . . looking for someone named Vanessa."

Vanessa turned and regarded the Hardys. "You may call me Ms. Kim," she said coolly. "The casting call for extras is the day after tomorrow. If you need more information about it, you can go online. Or you can get a flyer from one of the P.A.s. Now excuse me, but I'm very busy."

Frank stepped forward. "Actually, we wanted to talk to you about—"

"You two don't take no for an answer, do you?" Vanessa cut in. "Good for you! That's important in this business. But if you *really* want to be an actor, I'd do something about that haircut," she said, pointing to Joe. "As for you," she said to Frank, "have you considered a new image? Maybe all-black, kind of a young Goth thing?"

"Wait, what?" Joe ran a hand through his hair.

Frank glanced down at his jeans and plain yellow T-shirt. "Okay, well, uh . . . we wanted to talk to you about that zombie photo that was all over the Internet," he said. "Someone texted it to your phone from our friend Madison's phone. Was it you, Ms. Kim?"

Vanessa raised one eyebrow. "Excuse me?"

"We found your phone number on Madison's phone," Joe added.

"Fine. Whatever. So I got ahold of her picture and sent it around. It's my job to make sure the public is aware of anything and everything related to *Zombie Mania*," Vanessa said matter-of-factly.

Yes! Frank thought. Vanessa Kim was about to confess.

"So you're a publicist?" Frank asked her.

Vanessa smiled. "Isn't it obvious?"

"Did you arrange the whole thing from beginning to end?" Joe piped up. "Like, you hired someone to be the pretend zombie in Madison's picture?"

"No. But that's actually not a bad idea!" Vanessa pulled out her phone and began typing. "Note to self: Hire talent to impersonate zombies running around Bayport," she murmured as she typed.

Frank frowned. Vanessa had just admitted that she'd texted Madison's photo to herself and spread it around for publicity.

But she'd also claimed she'd had nothing to do with the zombies themselves.

Frank and Joe knew for sure now that the second zombie—the jogging-trail zombie—was Adam. Adam had said so himself.

So who was the zombie in Madison's photo?

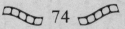

10

Secret File #12: Solved!

Did you know that according to one legend, you can make a zombie return to the grave by feeding it salt?" Frank told Joe.

"Hmm?" Joe stared at himself in their bedroom mirror. *More makeup,* he thought. He picked up their mom's brown eye shadow and smeared it across his forehead. He smudged it to make it look more like decaying flesh.

"And did you know that according to another legend, zombies aren't dead humans at all but souls

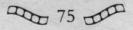

that are trapped in bottles? Then people buy the bottles for good luck and stuff?" Frank went on.

Joe turned around. Frank was sitting at his desk, poring intently over a thick paperback book.

"Okay, *what* are you reading?" Joe asked him curiously.

Frank held up the book. The title on the cover was *Zombies 101: Facts, Tips, and Tricks.*

Joe sighed. It was just before nine o'clock on Thursday night. The *Zombie Mania* casting call was

in exactly fourteen hours. Why wasn't Frank practicing, like he was?

Joe glanced down at the pile of clothes heaped on the floor. They were mostly old Halloween costumes that he had pulled from a trunk in the attic. He had been trying on different combinations all night to create the perfect zombie persona.

"There's a lot of great information about zombies in here," Frank remarked. "It's helping me to, you know, get into a zombie mind-set. For tomorrow's audition." He added, "It's giving me some new ideas about our case, too."

Joe turned back to the mirror and tried to imitate one of Tico's scary zombie expressions. "Like what?"

"Like, maybe we're looking at this wrong. Like, maybe we should be focusing more on the Why than the Who or the When or the other *W*s," Frank replied.

"How did your book make you decide that?" Joe asked, confused.

"Well . . . *real* zombies don't have a Why. The zombies I've been reading about don't have brains. And if they don't have brains, how can they have motives and reasons for doing stuff, right?" Frank said. "But our zombie *does* have a brain. Our zombie has a Why. We just have to figure out what it is."

"Oooo-kay." Speaking of brains, Frank's own brain sometimes worked in mysterious ways. But he did have a point. "I think I know what you're talking about. Sort of. So how do we figure out our zombie's Why?"

Frank opened a desk drawer and pulled out a notebook and pen. "Let's make a list of all the possible reasons why. Why would someone pretend to be a zombie?"

Joe started walking toward Frank so he could help with the list. He stopped and switched to a zombielike stagger. He had to stay in character.

"Number one Why: wanting to scare people," Joe suggested, peering over Frank's shoulder.

Frank wrote this down. "Definitely. There's also wanting attention, like Madison. And being obsessed with zombies, like Tico."

Joe scrunched up his face, trying to think. He felt as though he were missing an important Why.

He peered down at his zombie outfit. And touched the zombie goop on his face.

And then it came to him.

"I just thought of a new Why," Joe announced. "Wanting to be an extra in *Zombie Mania*!"

Frank nodded. "Yes! Maybe our suspect wanted to be in the movie so badly that he decided to rehearse his zombie moves in the park," he said, scribbling furiously.

"Or *her* zombie moves," Joe corrected Frank. "Of everyone we know, who thinks she already has a part in *Zombie Mania*? Who had T-shirts made up? And who would be super-embarrassed if she *didn't* get the part?"

Frank's eyes grew enormous. "Oh, yeah. *Melissa.*"

The next morning at eleven there was a long line of young zombie wannabes at the *Zombie Mania* casting call. Frank and Joe found Melissa and Todd standing right up front.

Melissa and Todd were both in zombie makeup and costume. Melissa's costume was a long gray wig and a baggy black dress. Todd's was denim overalls and a ripped-up flannel shirt.

"Hey, Melissa. Hey, Todd," Joe called out. "We finally figured out who the zombie in Madison's

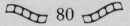

picture was. We wanted you guys to be the first to know!"

Melissa glared at him. "You're just trying to cut in line, Joe Hardy. Go away!"

"Not until you fess up, Melissa. We know it was you," Frank spoke up.

"What?" Melissa looked shocked. Actually, she looked more nervous than shocked. *Yeah, she's definitely our culprit,* Joe thought.

"You were practicing in West Meadow to get ready for today. You couldn't stand the thought of not being an extra," Frank said to Melissa.

Melissa's jaw dropped. "Seriously? *I* don't need to practice. *I* am a professional!" she said indignantly.

Joe was about to respond, when something caught his eye.

Todd was wearing red-and-black sneakers.

The zombie in Madison's picture had been wearing red-and-black sneakers.

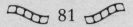 81

"You?" Joe said to Todd, surprised. *"You're* the zombie Madison saw?"

Todd flushed. "Uh, yeah. *I'm* the zombie."

"Todd! Stop talking right this second!" Melissa ordered him.

"It's okay, Melissa," Todd said with a sigh. "Melissa was worried that I wouldn't get a part in the movie," he explained to Joe and Frank. "She wanted us both to be extras. So she told me I had to dress up like a zombie and rehearse every day. She told me to pick a spot in the park where no one would see me."

"But Madison *did* see him, and she took his picture, and then the picture ended up all over the Internet," Melissa blurted out.

"Sorry to cause all this trouble," Todd apologized to the brothers.

A woman with a silver clipboard walked up to Frank and Joe. "You two boys ready for the casting

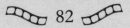 82

call? Come with me. I'm Maria, one of the assistant directors."

"But they cut in line!" Melissa wailed.

That night Joe and Frank went up to their tree house to wrap up the case—and their day.

Their day had been incredibly exciting. They hadn't gotten the acting parts as zombie extras. But they'd gotten to talk to Maria and another woman about why they wanted to be in the movie. They'd even gotten to meet Raj Kureshi for about two seconds!

Three kids had been cast for the zombie parts: Tico, Phil, and an older girl from the middle school. Joe and Frank were really, really psyched for Tico and Phil. They couldn't wait until next summer, when they could see their friends on the big screen.

Frank walked up to the dry-erase board. He

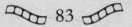

used his sleeve to wipe away the messy, jumbled old notes. Then he wrote:

Who: Todd

What: He pretended to be a zombie.

When: Tuesday morning

Where: Bayport Park, West Meadow,
    near the mayor statue

Why: Melissa said he had to rehearse
    being a zombie . . . or else!

How: He put on zombie clothes and
    makeup and left zombie footprints in
    the dirt.

Frank turned to Joe. "Oh, yeah. I almost forgot to tell you! Phil said he's going to throw a zombie party soon, to celebrate. Tico's helping out with decorations and food."

"Food?" Joe grinned. "You mean, like, human-flesh cookies? And human-flesh cupcakes?"

"Ewwwwww," Frank groaned.

The two boys cracked up.

SECRET FILES CASE #12: SOLVED!

FRANK AND JOE ARE MAKING THEIR OWN ZOMBIE MOVIE. . . .

Lights, camera—action!

Must . . . eat . . . human . . . Flesh!

Yummmmmm . . .

Boys, do you have any laundry for me?

Cut!

A SHORT WHILE LATER . . .

Chet! Mom says you have to come home!

Sorry, Frank.

GROAN!

Okay, we'll finish tomorrow.

Can I be in your monster movie? Pleeeeease?

Join Zeus and his friends as they set off on the adventure of a lifetime.

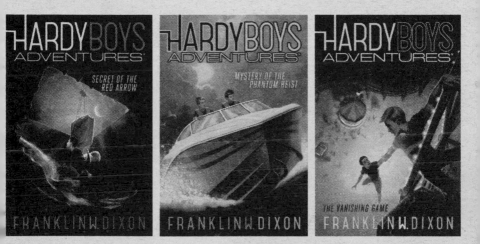